The Adventure

Hi! I'm Jackie. I'm an archaeologist. I study ancient treasures to learn about the past.

My big adventure began when I found an eight-sided stone in the center of a golden shield. The stone was a magical charm—a talisman!

Legend says that twelve talismans are scattered around the globe. Each one has a picture of an animal on it. And each one holds a different kind of magic. All twelve talismans together have incredible power!

An evil group called The Dark Hand wants to use the power of the talismans to rule the Earth! That's why I have to find all the talismans first.

I already have the rooster, ox, and snake talismans hidden in a safe place. The sheep talisman was really hard to track down. But I finally did.

Now I just have to travel halfway across the world to get it!

A PARACHUTE PRESS BOOK

TM and © 2002 Adelaide Productions, Inc. All Rights Reserved.

Published by Grosset & Dunlap, a division of Penguin Putnam Books for Young Readers, New York. GROSSET & DUNLAP is a trademark of Penguin Putnam, Inc. Published simultaneously in Canada. Printed in U.S.A.

No part of this book may be used or reproduced in any manner whatsoever without written permission of the publisher. For information, write to Grosset & Dunlap, a division of Penguin Putnam Books For Young Readers, 345 Hudson Street, New York, NY 10014, Attn: Permissions Department

Library of Congress Cataloging-in-Publication Data
Slack, David
  Shendu escapes / a novelization by Jim Thomas.
    p. cm. — (Jackie Chan adventures; #5)
  "A Parachute Press book."
  Based on the teleplay "Project A, for Astral," written by David Slack.
  Summary: An archaeologist seeking to bring together twelve magical talismans must battle the evil Shendu, whose spirit possessed Chan's eleven-year-old niece when the sheep talisman caused her to leave her body.
  [1. Talismans—Fiction. 2. Magic—Fiction. 3. Astral projection—Fiction. 4. Martial artists—Fiction.] I. Thomas, Jim. II. Title. III. Jackie Chan Adventures; no. 5.

PZ7.S62882 Sh 2002
[Fic]—dc21   2001040896

ISBN 0-448-42668-4
A B C D E F G H I J

JACKIE CHAN

ADVENTURES ™ #5

Shendu Escapes!

A novelization by Jim Thomas
based on the teleplay "Project A, for Astral"
written by David Slack

Grosset & Dunlap

Chapter 1

"Almost . . . there," Jackie grunted as he climbed onto the roof of a speeding freight train. He was in Turkey. The train was on its way to a city called Istanbul.

It had taken Jackie two months to track down the sheep talisman. But soon his search would be over.

Jackie opened a hatch in the train's roof and jumped down into the car below. He found himself surrounded by wooden crates. He spotted the one he was looking for right away. It had ISTANBUL stamped on it.

Yes! Jackie thought. He used a crowbar to pry open the box.

"Finally, the sheep talisman," Jackie whispered. He picked up the small eight-sided stone and stared at it. There was ancient Chinese writing on one side. A pale green sheep was painted on the other. The sheep was one of the twelve symbols of the Chinese zodiac.

Jackie grinned. "Jackie had a little lamb," he said, and he dropped the talisman into his pocket.

Then he heard a strange fluttering sound. He turned and saw six ninja warriors standing behind him.

Shadowkhan! Jackie thought. The Shadowkhan were part of an evil group called The Dark Hand. The Dark Hand would do anything to get the talismans. They wanted to use the powers of the twelve talismans to rule the world!

Jackie was helping a top-secret law enforcement group called Section Thirteen. It was Jackie's job to find the talismans first.

Jackie hoped the Shadowkhan hadn't seen him hide the sheep talisman. "It's not here," he said. "Can you believe it?"

The Shadowkhan did not reply. Instead, they threw something at Jackie.

Jackie ducked. Six ninja stars landed

in the crate above his head. "Guess not," he said.

The Shadowkhan drew their swords.

Clang! Jackie blocked one sword with his crowbar. Another sword just missed his head.

Jackie wedged the crowbar into a nearby crate. Quickly, he pulled off the lid and used it as a shield.

I've got to get out of here, he thought. He backed toward the hatch. But the Shadowkhan were slashing his shield to pieces!

Jackie kicked the nearest two Shadowkhan and knocked them over. Then he jumped onto a stack of crates and pulled himself through the opening in the roof. He ran on top of the cars toward the front of the train. But suddenly Jackie was surrounded by even more ninjas!

Just as they began to attack, Jackie's cell phone rang. He blocked a punch and answered the phone at the same time.

"Hello?" he gasped.

"Jackie, help!" It was Jade, Jackie's eleven-year-old niece.

"What's wrong?" Jackie asked.

"*Never* leave me with Uncle again!" Jade said. Jade was staying with Uncle while Jackie was away.

Uncle lived in an apartment above his antique shop in San Francisco, California.

"We only eat mung beans and rice," Jade said. "And I'm bored!"

"Jade, I'm a little busy right now," Jackie said. He kicked a Shadowkhan in the chest. He blocked another punch.

"But Uncle's no fun at all," Jade complained. "I wanted to go to the new Melvin World amusement park. Uncle said, 'Roller coasters are bad for digestion!'"

Jackie gasped as a sword sliced his pocket wide open. The sheep talisman dropped out, and a Shadowkhan grabbed it.

"No!" Jackie cried.

"I know!" said Jade. "Can you believe it?"

Jackie looked up. Above him was a shiny black helicopter. The Shadowkhan threw the talisman to someone in the aircraft. It was Finn, an enforcer from The Dark Hand.

Another enforcer, named Ratso, stood next to him.

Jade was still talking over the phone. "Promise we'll go as soon as you get home?"

"Yes!" Jackie said. He had to hang up. "Whatever! I promise! Good-bye!"

Above Jackie, the helicopter was flying away. All of the Shadowkhan around him disappeared in clouds of mist.

I lost the sheep talisman to The Dark Hand! Jackie thought miserably. What am I going to do?

Inside the helicopter, Finn and Ratso were celebrating. They had the sheep talisman! They called their boss, Valmont, on their video phone. Valmont's face appeared on the tiny TV screen.

"Mr. Valmont!" Finn said. He held up the sheep talisman proudly. "I've got it!"

"And Jackie Chan?" Valmont asked coldly.

Finn grinned. "We'll take care of him right now," he said.

From down below, Jackie watched the helicopter fly away. He groaned. Now The Dark Hand had the sheep talisman!

Then Jackie heard the helicopter fire missiles. With a roar, the missiles zoomed past the train. Jackie gasped as he watched where they were going. Straight ahead was a bridge that stretched across a deep canyon.

Ka-boom! The missiles hit the bridge, and the bridge exploded!

Oh, no! Jackie thought. Now the train is going to go off a cliff!

Chapter 2

I have to get off this train! Jackie thought.

"Help!" a man cried out.

It was the train's engineer! Jackie hurried to the front of the train. He leaned over the side of the first car and peered inside.

The engineer was staring out his window. The edge of the cliff was only a few feet away!

"Jump!" Jackie yelled.

But the engineer was too scared to move.

Jackie grabbed the man's shirt and pulled him out the window. The engineer dropped safely to the ground.

But before Jackie could jump, too, the train started to go over the cliff! Jackie raced toward the back of the train. When he reached the last car, he jumped off.

Jackie sailed through the air—and grabbed hold of the cliffside. He dangled from the rocks, trying not to look at the canyon below him.

Could this day get any worse? Jackie wondered.

Then he heard Finn and Ratso's helicopter flying straight toward him. If it got too close, the blades would chop him to pieces!

"Bad day, bad day, bad day, bad day!" Jackie cried. He scrambled up the cliff as fast as he could.

"Yaaaahhhh!" he cried as the helicopter passed very close to him. Then he had an idea. This was his chance to get the talisman back!

When the helicopter made another close pass, Jackie leaped inside.

Finn and Ratso turned around. Finn was driving the helicopter. He was also holding the sheep talisman.

"Chan!" Ratso cried. He came after Jackie.

"Yaaaahhh!" Jackie blocked Ratso's punch. He kicked the talisman right out of Finn's hand at the same time.

Jackie caught it. "One-stop shopping!" he joked.

Ratso didn't laugh. He pulled what looked like a sword handle from his pocket. Then he pressed a button on the handle. *Bzzzzz!* An electric blade appeared.

Ratso slashed at Jackie—and missed. The electric sword drilled through the helicopter's controls!

"No!" Finn cried.

"Uh-oh," Ratso said.

The helicopter was in big trouble. Jackie knew he had to get out of there. He grabbed a rope off the floor. Then he went to the helicopter door and leaned out of the aircraft.

Jackie hooked the rope around the bottom of the helicopter. Then he swung to the ground and skidded to a stop. He watched the smoking helicopter fly away.

I have the sheep talisman! Jackie thought happily.

His latest job for Section Thirteen was done.

Now he could go home and get some rest!

Chapter 3

Five days later, Jackie stood outside his uncle's antique shop. It was called Uncle's Rare Finds. At last, he was back in San Francisco! He had been traveling a long time and all he wanted to do was go to sleep.

First, though, he needed to show the sheep talisman to Uncle. Then he and Jade would take it to Section Thirteen, where they both lived.

Jackie picked up his bags and

walked into the antique shop.

"Jackie!" Jade cried.

Jackie smiled and gave her a hug.

"I'm going to Melvin World!" Jade sang.

"Huh?" Jackie said, confused. Then he remembered Jade's phone call. "Oh, okay," Jackie said. He put down his bags. "But first let me get some sleep."

Jade frowned. "Awww," she said.

Uncle came out from the back room. "Jackie!" he called.

"Uncle!" Jackie said. He held out his arms for a hug.

Uncle shuffled past Jackie. He was more interested in Jackie's luggage. "What did you bring me?" Uncle asked.

Jackie knew what Uncle was looking for. He reached into his pocket. "I have the sheep talisman," he said.

"Good," Uncle said. He took the talisman. "Now we can do research."

"But, Uncle," Jackie said, "I'm very tired."

"Oh, I'm sorry," Uncle said. He held the talisman up to his ear. "Wait."

"What is it?" Jackie asked. "What do you hear?"

"I *hear. . .*," Uncle said slowly, "the sound of the sheep talisman *not* telling me what power it holds."

Uncle grabbed Jackie's wrist and dragged him toward the back room of the shop. "I *hear* the sound of our footsteps as we walk to my study to translate ancient writing!"

"Jackie, no!" Jade said. She grabbed his other arm. "Take me to Melvin World!"

"*Please,* Uncle," Jackie said. "I've been traveling for days! I escaped a train crash! I jumped from a helicopter!"

"That is why you must relax with some *good books,*" Uncle said firmly. He opened the door to the back room. Inside were stacks and stacks of dusty old books.

Jackie stared at them and groaned.

In another part of town, Finn and Ratso had also gotten home. They were with their boss, Valmont. Behind Valmont's desk was a statue of a dragon. The statue held the evil spirit of Shendu. Shendu was the real leader of The Dark Hand.

"Chan has another talisman?" Shendu asked. Its eyes glowed red in anger. "You are weak, Valmont. Your men are fools!"

Finn frowned. "Hey!" he said. "I don't have to take that from a *statue!*"

"I am not a statue," Shendu hissed. "I am a powerful demon sorcerer! Once, I ruled a huge empire. But some of my people tricked me. They cast a spell on me. It trapped me in this shape."

"Whoa," Ratso said.

"My power came from twelve magic talismans," Shendu said. "They were lost."

Finn sneered. "I bet you got robbed."

Shendu ignored him. "I need all twelve talismans. Only then will I be free!"

Valmont turned to his men. "And if we find the talismans, Shendu will give us more money and jewels than we ever dreamed of. That's worth taking orders from a statue, isn't it?" he growled.

"Yes, sir," Finn said quietly.

"Good," Valmont said. "Now it's time to visit our friend Jackie Chan again. Am I right?"

Ratso laughed. "You're right, boss," he said.

Valmont looked at Finn. "And you? Do you think it's a good idea?"

"For money and jewels . . ." Finn grinned nastily. "Oh, yeah."

Chapter 4

Back at the antique shop, Uncle tried to figure out the sheep talisman's power. Jackie tried not to fall asleep.

Uncle pointed to the writing on the talisman. "These symbols explain its power. We must translate them."

Jackie's eyes began to close.

Thwap! Uncle whacked Jackie's forehead with the talisman.

"Ow!" Jackie said. "Counting sheep makes me very sleepy!"

"One more thing," Uncle said. He put the talisman into a small red box. "We must keep the talisman in this magic box. It will be safe there."

"One *more* thing!" Uncle said to Jackie. "Stay awake! You break many antiques when you sleepwalk."

"I don't sleepwalk!" said Jackie.

"So," Uncle said, "you break my antiques for *fun?*"

Jade had been watching them from the stairs. While Uncle and Jackie argued, Jade sneaked the talisman out of the box and ran upstairs with it.

"Jackie and Uncle will spend *weeks* looking in those dusty books," Jade said. "I'll figure out what the talisman does the easy way—by trying it out. Then Jackie can take me to Melvin

World!" She glanced at the sheep talisman. "I just hope this isn't the exploding head talisman!"

Jade squeezed the talisman, trying to get it to work. Nothing. She hit it on the floor. Still nothing. She kicked it. She bit it. Nothing, nothing.

Finally she stared at it in her hand and said, "Work already!"

Jade gasped when the sheep symbol glowed. Then a flash of light exploded from the talisman! Jade was thrown back onto the couch.

She tried to stand up. But instead of standing, she floated! Jade glanced over her shoulder. Wait a minute. . . .

Her body was still on the couch! What was going on?

"Oh, no!" Jade said. "I'm dead! I'm

a spirit or something!" She dove back into her body and opened her eyes. "So I'm *not* dead?" Jade wondered. She was very confused.

Jade slipped out of her body again. She floated to the ceiling. Her body was still stretched on the couch. The sheep talisman was in her right hand. It looked as if she was sleeping.

Then Jade realized what had happened. The talisman had given her the power to leave her body!

"Cool!" Jade said. "This must be . . . the *ghost* talisman! Jackie won't believe it!"

Jade floated down through the floor—just like a ghost. She flew into the dusty study where Jackie and Uncle were reading.

"Boo!" Jade said.

Jackie and Uncle didn't move.

"Hello? Can't you see me?" Jade asked. She waved her hands in front of Jackie's face. "No? Then you won't mind if I . . . touch your guts!"

Jade stuck her hands right through Jackie's stomach! She laughed. "This is way better than Melvin World! I'm going to have some fun at the park." Jade shot up through the ceiling and into the sky. "Yahoo!"

Finn and Ratso arrived at Uncle's Rare Finds. They had The Seeker with them. It was a large wand with four dragons on top. Each dragon pointed in a different direction. The Seeker could sense where the talismans were.

"This is a waste of time," Ratso said. "They've probably hidden it at Section Thirteen by now."

Finn held up The Seeker. One of the dragon's eyes glowed. It was the dragon closest to the store. "Or maybe not," Finn said with a grin.

Finn and Ratso sneaked into Uncle's shop. The Seeker led them upstairs. There, they found Jade sleeping on the couch. The sheep talisman was in her hand!

"No way!" Ratso whispered.

"*Yes* way," said Finn.

Finn plucked the talisman out of Jade's hand. Then he and Ratso left the shop. They hurried back to The Dark Hand headquarters.

Once there, Finn placed the sheep

talisman on Valmont's desk proudly.

"We had to fight Chan for this," Finn lied. "He threw a bus at us! But we still got it."

"Congratulations, Shendu," Valmont said. He tossed the talisman to the statue of Shendu.

The dragon statue had twelve empty slots on its body—one for each of the talismans.

Click! The sheep talisman landed in a slot.

The sheep symbol glowed. Then the entire talisman flashed. Shendu let out a loud, evil laugh. His spirit floated out of the statue!

"The sheep talisman frees my spirit form! It is a good start. But I must have all twelve talismans," Shendu said.

Ratso swallowed nervously. "But Chan already took some talismans to Section Thirteen. Finding Section Thirteen won't be easy. Taking the sheep talisman from a sleeping girl—*that* was easy."

Finn poked Ratso in the stomach. But it was too late.

Valmont frowned at his men. "Did that happen *before* or *after* Chan threw the bus at you?"

Finn and Ratso were embarrassed. They had been caught lying.

Shendu ignored them. "Maybe the child *wasn't* sleeping," he said. "Maybe she used the sheep talisman. If so, then her body is empty—and I can fill it!"

Chapter 5

It wasn't much fun being a ghost.

Jade was in the park. She had been playing tricks on her friends all day. But nobody could see or hear her.

She stuck her finger into a boy's nostril. "Eww!" she said. "Quit picking your nose!"

No one laughed. No one even knew she was there!

"This stinks," Jade said. "I'm out of here."

Jade flew back to Uncle's shop. Her body was still on the couch. Jackie was sleeping on the floor next to it. He must have come upstairs while I was at the park, Jade thought. Then she noticed that something was missing. . . .

"Where's the talisman?" Jade asked. "It's not in my body's hand!" She began to look around the room. Suddenly, a dragon-like creature appeared behind her.

"Whoa!" Jade said. "W-W-What are you?" She had never met Shendu before.

Shendu's eyes glowed an evil red. "I am your greatest fear!" he said. Then he zoomed past Jade and jumped into her body.

Jade's body sat up and opened her eyes. They were glowing red! Shendu had taken over Jade's body. It was Evil Jade!

Evil Jade nudged Jackie to wake him.

"Huh?" Jackie mumbled. "What?"

The red glow faded from Evil Jade's eyes. "Time to wake up," Evil Jade said.

The real Jade was still floating near the ceiling. "Get out of my body!" she yelled. She tried to dive into her body, but she just bounced off.

"Get out of there!" Jade cried. "Give me back my skin and bones!"

Evil Jade didn't listen. She helped Jackie to his feet. "You should not sleep on the floor, Uncle Jackie," she said.

Jackie yawned. "Right. We should get back to Section Thirteen."

Evil Jade grinned. "Yes," she said. "Section Thirteen."

"Jackieeee!" Uncle called from downstairs.

Jackie sighed. He and Evil Jade started downstairs.

The real Jade flew in front of Jackie. "Jackie, she's not me!" Jade cried. "You've got to listen!"

Jackie didn't stop. He walked right through Jade to the bottom of the stairs.

Evil Jade stopped for a moment. Her eyes glowed red. "Scream all you want," she told Jade. "No one can hear you."

The real Jade followed Evil Jade

into the kitchen. "I want my body back!" Jade cried. "Leave Jackie alone!"

Evil Jade smiled. She picked up a large knife.

Jade gasped. "Jackie, Jackie, Jackie!" she cried. "Look out!"

But Evil Jade used the knife to cut up an orange. Then she made some tea. She carried a tray into Uncle's study.

The real Jade followed her.

"Refreshments, anyone?" Evil Jade asked. "Orange slices and tea?"

Uncle and Jackie looked surprised.

"Wonderful!" Uncle said.

"Thank you, Jade," Jackie said. He picked up a cup of tea.

"It's probably poisoned!" the real Jade cried. "Don't drink it! Jackie, no!"

But it was no use. Jackie couldn't hear her. He took a sip of tea. Jade covered her eyes.

"Mmm," Jackie said. "Delicious."

"And good for you, too," Evil Jade said.

Jade uncovered one eye. "Ugh!" she said. "Jackie, she is *so* not me! I'm never that nice. Can't you tell she's an evil spirit?"

Jade thought for a moment. Why *is* evil me being so nice?

"Excuse me. I wish to go to Section Thirteen now," Evil Jade said to Jackie.

"Section Thirteen," Jade repeated. "That's it! She wants the other talismans! Evil me is working for The Dark Hand!"

Chapter 6

Jackie picked up the phone to call Captain Augustus Black. Captain Black was a friend of Jackie's. He was in charge of Section Thirteen.

Captain Black answered the phone. "Black," he said.

"It's Jackie," Jackie said. "Can you send someone to get Jade and bring her to Section Thirteen?"

"Are you all right, Jackie?" Captain Black asked.

"I'm fine," Jackie said. "I'm just tired. And I haven't been able to spend much time with Jade. She really wants to go to Melvin World—"

"No need to say any more, Jackie," Captain Black said. "I'll be right over to pick her up."

Twenty minutes later, someone knocked at the door. It was Captain Black. He was there to pick up Jade.

Evil Jade smiled. She climbed into Captain Black's car, and they drove off.

"No!" the real Jade cried. "You can't let her go to Section Thirteen!"

Just then Uncle yelled, "Hot-cha!" He was looking at a book. "I've discovered the sheep talisman's magic power," he said. "It frees the spirit from the body!"

"Yes, yes, yes, yes, yes!" Jade cheered.

"Great," said Jackie. "Night-night." He closed his eyes and started snoring.

"One more thing!" Uncle said loudly.

Jackie snapped awake.

"Spirits can pass through walls," Uncle said. "But they cannot be seen or heard."

"*Duh,*" Jade muttered.

"*Unless,*" Uncle continued, "they enter a person's *dreams.*"

"Dreams?" Jade said. She looked at Jackie. He was asleep again! Now she could explain everything to him.

But before Jade could dive into

Jackie's dream, Uncle thwacked him on the forehead.

"Ouch!" Jackie said.

"One *more* thing," Uncle said. He held out a broom. "You forgot to sweep the store."

Jackie rubbed his forehead. Uncle had thwacked him a lot today. His forehead was getting sore!

Jackie took the broom. He started sweeping. But he was tired. He swept very slowly.

"Come on, come on," Jade said. "Sweep faster, Jackie!"

But Jackie swept more and more slowly. Finally, he stopped.

"Huh?" Jade said. She looked at Jackie's face. He'd fallen asleep again! Standing up!

"All right!" Jade cheered. She dove into Jackie's head—and into his dream!

In his dream, Jackie was sweeping the shop. Everything in the store was giant-sized. All the colors were glowing.

"Jackie, can you see me?" Jade asked.

"Can't talk now, Jade," Jackie answered. "I have to sweep."

Yes! Jade thought. He *can* see me!

Then a loud voice said, "Jackieeee!"

Uncle was standing over them. But Uncle was a giant! Giant Uncle thwacked Jackie on the forehead.

"Ow!" Jackie said, tumbling through the air. He landed on the roof of a pink train. He started to sweep it.

Jade floated after him. "Jackie!" she cried. "You have to listen to me. You're dreaming!"

"Not now," Jackie said. "Got to sweep the train."

The train started to move.

"Oh, no!" Jackie said. He started running.

Suddenly, Jade was kicked out of Jackie's dream! She was back in Uncle's real shop.

What happened? Jade wondered. Then she figured it out. Jackie was sleepwalking! He had started moving in real life. And Jade hadn't moved with him.

Jackie was walking away. Jade followed him. "Stand still!" she called out. She dove into his dream again.

Jackie was still running on top of the pink train.

Jade floated beside him. "You're dreaming," she said. "*And* you're sleepwalking!"

"I don't sleepwalk," Jackie said.

Jade floated in front of Jackie. She held up her arms. "Jackie," Jade said. "You're dreaming. But I'm real! I took the sheep talisman and got all ghosty. Then an evil spirit took over my body. Now evil me is going to Section Thirteen with Captain Black. She's going to steal the other talismans you've found!"

"That's crazy, Jade," Jackie said. "*You're* crazy."

"I can prove everything," Jade said. "Look in Uncle's magic box. The

41

sheep talisman is gone. Now *wake up!*"

Jackie opened his eyes. "The talisman!" he cried.

He rushed to Uncle's study and opened the red magic box. The talisman was gone!

Jackie gasped. "My dream was real!" he said. "And The Dark Hand has captured the sheep talisman *again!*"

Chapter 7

"Uncle!" Jackie cried. "Come quickly! The sheep talisman is gone!"

Jade did a little floating dance in the air. "I'm the bomb," she sang.

"Where is the talisman?" Uncle asked.

"This will sound crazy, but . . ." Jackie began.

"Jade took the talisman," Uncle finished. "She is trapped in spirit form. And an evil spirit—someone called Shendu—walks in her body."

Jackie was surprised. "Right," he said.

"Evil Jade is like a wolf in sheep's clothing," Uncle said. "You find the sheep. I will find a spell to trap the wolf."

Jade grinned. "Go, Uncle!"

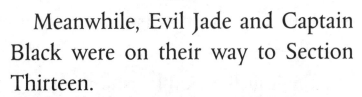

Meanwhile, Evil Jade and Captain Black were on their way to Section Thirteen.

"We're almost there, Jade," Captain Black said. He held out a blindfold. "Put this on, please."

The location of Section Thirteen was a secret. Even Jackie didn't know where it was.

Evil Jade grinned. "At last," she

said, and she happily put on the blindfold.

A few minutes later, the car stopped.

"Okay," Captain Black said. "You can look now!"

Evil Jade lowered the blindfold. Her grin disappeared when she saw all the rides and games. Captain Black hadn't taken her to Section Thirteen. He'd taken her to Melvin World!

"Surprise!" Captain Black said. "Jackie told me that you wanted to come here. So I thought I'd bring you. Are you happy?" he asked.

Evil Jade wasn't happy, but she had to pretend she was. "Yes," she answered.

Evil Jade and Captain Black entered the park and soon got onto the roller coaster. Then Captain Black's cell phone rang.

"Hello?" he said into the phone.

"Captain Black," Jackie said, "you're in terrible danger. Jade is evil!" He and the real Jade were hurrying to the amusement park.

The roller coaster started to move. "I know she's a handful, Jackie," Captain Black said. "But *evil?*" He laughed and hung up.

The roller coaster zipped up and then down a steep track.

"Whee!" Captain Black laughed. He was having fun!

Evil Jade wasn't. She crossed her arms and frowned.

She frowned on every single ride they went on.

Soon a voice sounded over the loudspeaker. "Melvin World is now closing."

"Aw," Captain Black said.

"Finally!" Evil Jade grumbled.

Just then, Jackie ran up to Captain Black. The real Jade was floating beside him.

"Captain Black!" Jackie cried. "Get away from her. She's not really Jade!"

Evil Jade pinched a spot on Captain Black's shoulder.

Captain Black gasped and fell to the ground.

"Who *are* you?" Jackie asked.

Evil Jade's eyes glowed red. "Your worst nightmare," she hissed. She moved to attack Jackie.

Jackie held her back with one arm.

"Jade!" Jackie said. "Stop that! Or I'll . . . I'll give you a spanking!"

Evil Jade laughed. "Go ahead. This isn't *my* body."

She tried to kick Jackie. But she wasn't strong enough to hurt him. "I'm in the body of a weak little girl!" Evil Jade mumbled.

"Hey!" cried the real Jade. "I am *not* weak!"

Evil Jade turned and ran into the Melvin World Fun House.

Jackie and the real Jade hurried after her.

Once inside, Jackie spotted Evil Jade right away.

He tried to grab her. But he

banged his head on something. "Ow!" he cried. He'd walked right into a mirror.

Jackie looked around. There were hundreds of mirrors in the room. And Jackie could see Evil Jade's reflection in every one.

Then Evil Jade disappeared. And suddenly, Jackie found himself surrounded by Shadowkhan warriors!

Chapter 8

Jackie had to kick, block, and punch his way out of the Fun House. He had to find Evil Jade.

Quickly, Jackie made his way to the roof of the Fun House to get a view of the whole park. He spotted a huge Melvin World sign. Jackie climbed to the top of it.

The Shadowkhan saw Jackie, and they climbed after him. But they were too heavy for the sign. With a crack, the big sign began to fall!

"Whoa!" Jackie cried. He jumped and flipped into the air. He landed on the tracks of the roller coaster.

Almost immediately, the Shadow-khan flipped onto the tracks, too. Jackie was surrounded.

With a quick kick, he sent one ninja flying. But more were closing in.

Evil Jade was watching the fight from the ground. She climbed the stairs to the roller coaster. When she reached the top, she headed for the controls, then turned them on.

The real Jade was floating beside her. "What are you doing?" she asked.

Evil Jade didn't answer. A train of roller coaster cars pulled up. Evil Jade got into the first car.

"Hey!" Jade called out. Then she realized what Evil Jade was up to. Jackie was fighting the ninjas on the roller coaster tracks. And Evil Jade was going to run him down!

Meanwhile, Jackie was spinning, ducking, and kicking. The Shadow-khan were fighting him from all sides!

Then Jackie heard a rumbling sound. The ninjas began jumping off the track. Jackie looked over his shoulder. A roller coaster car was almost on top of him!

Thinking fast, Jackie jumped off the track, too. He landed on the track below—where the Shadowkhan were!

A warrior leaped toward him.

Jackie ducked, and the Shadow-khan fell off the track. Another one came at him, and Jackie punched the ninja in the stomach.

Then two more Shadowkhan attacked Jackie at the same time— one on each side of him. Jackie jumped up into a split kick.

"Heeeeya!" Jackie called. His kick smashed each Shadowkhan in the chest.

Jackie landed in a crouch, ready for more. Then his cell phone rang. He answered it. "I'm busy!" Jackie yelled.

A Shadowkhan popped up behind him. Jackie elbowed the ninja's chin, toppling the warrior.

"Jackie," Uncle said over the

phone, "I found a spell to send Shendu back to his statue. A very good spell! Please put Evil Jade on phone."

Jackie looked out over the roller coaster tracks. Evil Jade was riding in the first car. She was about to pass right under him!

Jackie jumped and landed in the seat behind Evil Jade. He wrapped her in a bear hug and held the phone to her ear.

"Hello?" Uncle said. He began chanting the spell. "*Yu Mo Goo Guai Fi Di Ziao. Yu Mo Goo Guai Fi Di Ziao. . . .*"

"*Noooo!*" Evil Jade howled. Red beams of light shot out of her eyes and mouth.

Shendu's spirit form flew over the city and returned to the dragon statue behind Valmont's desk.

The statue's eyes glowed red.

"Cannot . . . break . . . free!" Shendu grunted. "Blasted spell!"

Valmont was sitting at his desk. "Shendu," he said. "Back so soon?"

The demon sorcerer growled.

Back at the amusement park, Jackie sat in the roller coaster. He was holding Jade's sleeping body in his arms.

"Jade!" He shook her gently. "Jade!"

Jade floated next to Jackie. She was still in her spirit form. "Coming!" she called.

Then she dove into her body and

opened her eyes. "I'm back!" she said with a grin.

Jackie smiled with relief. Then he frowned. "Jade," he said. "We lost the sheep talisman to The Dark Hand."

Jade ducked her head. "And it's all my fault," she said.

Jackie saw how sorry Jade was. He smiled. "But," he said gently, "I guess it's also because of you that the rest of the talismans are still safe at Section Thirteen."

"That's right!" Jade cried, feeling much better.

The Dark Hand may have the sheep talisman for now, she thought with a grin. But one day, *I'm* going to help get it back!

A letter to you from Jackie

Dear Friends,

In _Shendu Escapes!_ Jade swipes the sheep talisman from a magic box so she can learn its secret power. Jade thinks if she discovers the power right away, I'll have time to take her to Melvin World because I won't be busy translating the ancient writing on the talisman.

But Jade is thinking only of herself when she takes the talisman. She does not consider what might happen to others when she unleashes the power on her own.

In the end, the sheep talisman is lost to The Dark Hand. And Jade learns a great lesson: sometimes it's more important to think of others before thinking of yourself.

This is a lesson that I try to remember every day. I think part of my success comes from the fact that I'm always thinking of my fans when I make my movies. In fact, they're the number one reason why I make films! I don't believe in giving the audience only half of what a Jackie movie can be. Each film has to be just as special as the one before it.

But that's not the only way I think of others. I

always make an extra effort to be nice to people. I treat people courteously and with respect. I also believe it is important to help people whenever possible. One way I do this is by participating in charitable events and dedicating time, effort, and heart to my own charitable foundation.

A while back, I started the Jackie Chan Foundation to raise money for scholarships and for hospital expansion. I also contribute to a group that helps disabled people who are living at home, as well as donate to many other good causes.

There are lots of things <u>you</u> can do to help others. It can be something as simple as helping a friend with his or her homework or volunteering at a hospital after school.

If you want to become part of a big charity that will help lots of people, you can do that, too! Just ask your parents or your teacher for help. They can tell you what charities are out there, and show you how to get involved once you pick one.

The best part about thinking of other people first is that it makes you feel good about yourself. So keep that in mind the next time you have the chance to do something nice for someone else—then do it!

Find out what happens in the next book

#6 A New Enemy

Jackie finds the rabbit talisman in the shell of a turtle named Aesop. But Jackie's got more than a talisman to rescue when Aesop is captured by a man who's hungry for turtle soup!

As seen on Kids WB

JACKIE CHAN ADVENTURES™ #6

Inside: A letter to you from Jackie!

A New Enemy

Cool trading card inside!

JACKIE CHAN ADVENTURES™

SHARE THE ADVENTURE!

Jackie Chan now has a game that lets you experience the fun and excitement of the TV show yourself. Take on the sinister bad guys of The Dark Hand as you race to retrieve the magic talismans.

Available At Toys R Us

Cardinal Industries , Inc. L.I.C. NY 11101